Put Beginning Readers on the Right Track with
ALL ABOARD READING™

The All Aboard Reading series is especially designed for beginning readers. Written by noted authors and illustrated in full color, these are books that children really want to read—books to excite their imagination, expand their interests, make them laugh, and support their feelings. With fiction and nonfiction stories that are high interest and curriculum-related, All Aboard Reading books offer something for every young reader. And with four different reading levels, the All Aboard Reading series lets you choose which books are most appropriate for your children and their growing abilities.

Picture Readers
Picture Readers have super-simple texts, with many nouns appearing as rebus pictures. At the end of each book are 24 flash cards—on one side is a rebus picture; on the other side is the written-out word.

Station Stop 1
Station Stop 1 books are best for children who have just begun to read. Simple words and big type make these early reading experiences more comfortable. Picture clues help children to figure out the words on the page. Lots of repetition throughout the text helps children to predict the next word or phrase—an essential step in developing word recognition.

Station Stop 2
Station Stop 2 books are written specifically for children who are reading with help. Short sentences make it easier for early readers to understand what they are reading. Simple plots and simple dialogue help children with reading comprehension.

Station Stop 3
Station Stop 3 books are perfect for children who are reading alone. With longer text and harder words, these books appeal to children who have mastered basic reading skills. More complex stories captivate children who are ready for more challenging books.

In addition to All Aboard Reading books, look for All Aboard Math Readers™ (fiction stories that teach math concepts children are learning in school) and All Aboard Science Readers™ (nonfiction books that explore the most fascinating science topics in age-appropriate language).

All Aboard for happy reading!

To my American grandmothers,
Marnie and Laura, who always save room
for my books on their coffee table—B.A.

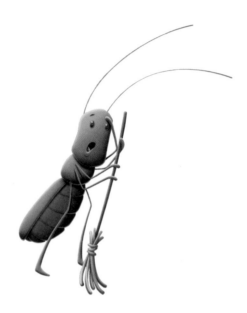

Library of Congress Cataloging-in-Publication Data

Harvey, Jayne.
  Busy bugs / by Jayne Harvey ; illustrated by Bernard Adnet.
    p. cm. — (All aboard math reader. Station stop 1)
    Summary: The busy bugs arrange themselves in different ways to make a show.
    [1. Pattern perception—Fiction. 2. Insects—Fiction. 3. Counting. 4. Stories in
rhyme.] I. Adnet, Bernard, ill. II. Title. III. Series.
  PZ8.3.H2587Bu 2003
  [E]—dc21
                                                                2003004837

ISBN 0-448-43159-9 (pbk)   A B C D E F G H I J
ISBN 0-448-43234-X (GB)   A B C D E F G H I J

BUSY BUGS

A Book About Patterns

By Jayne Harvey
Illustrated by Bernard Adnet

Grosset & Dunlap • New York

The busy bugs are moving fast.
A special day has come at last.

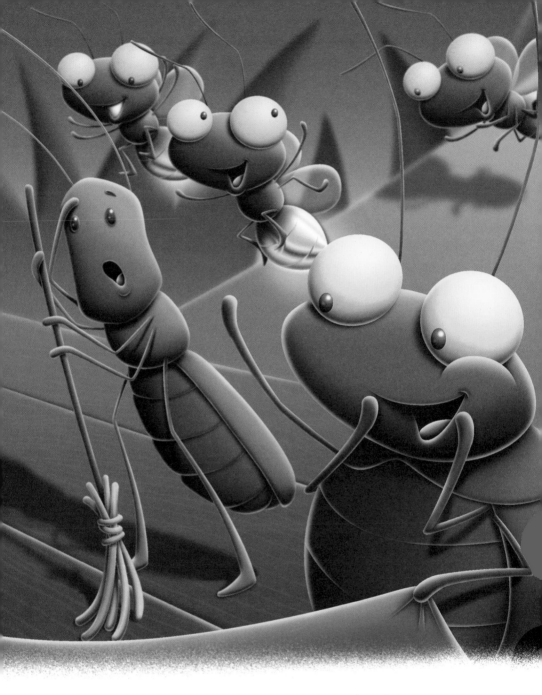

They make patterns as they go,
getting ready for the show.

The ladybugs
must shine their spots.

Each red wing
has three black dots.

Butterflies clean
their matching wings.

"Oh, how pretty!"
a cricket sings.

The spiders go
around and around.

They spin their webs
down to the ground.

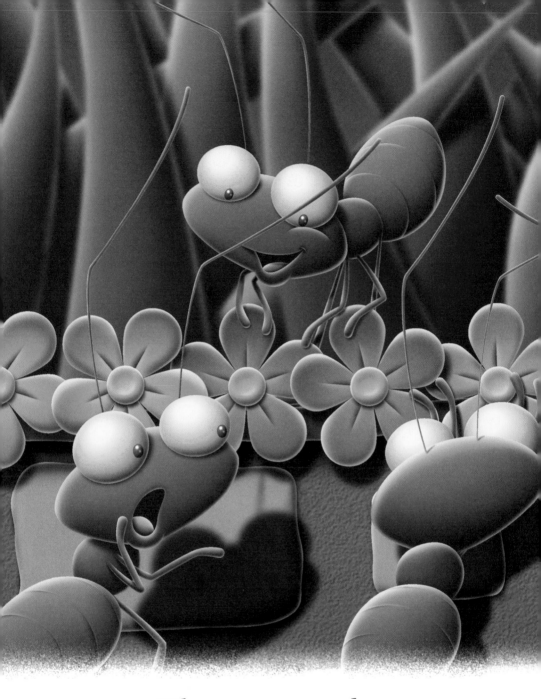

The ants spend
many busy hours

making patterns
with the flowers.

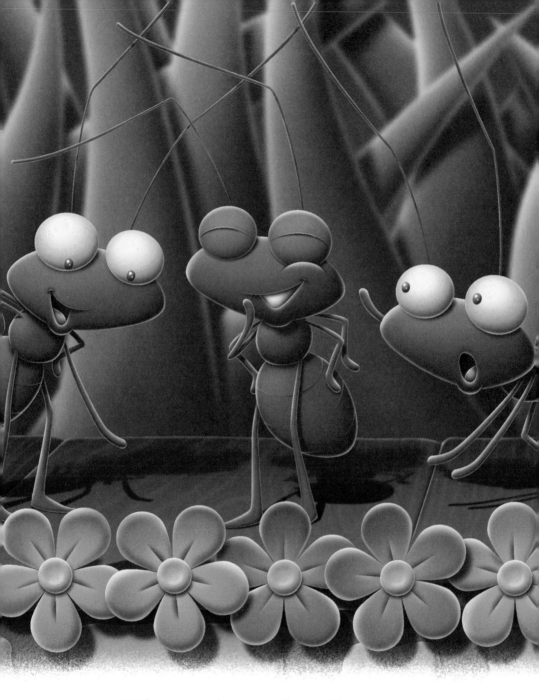

They place the flowers
two by two.

14

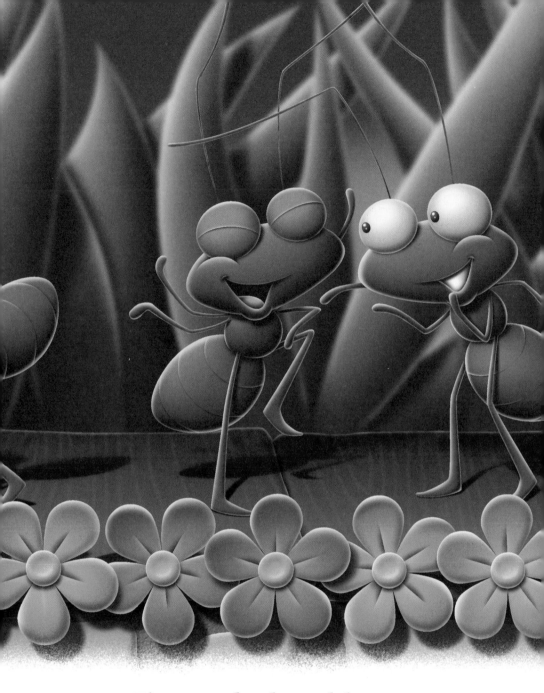

First red, then blue.

Then red, then blue.

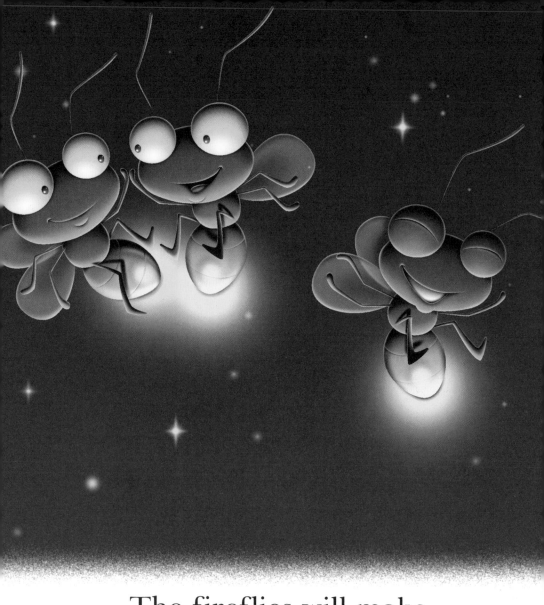

The fireflies will make
things bright.
Each firefly shines
with yellow light.

They make a pattern
just for fun.
Two lights, then one.
Two lights, then one.

Now the bugs are ready to go.

It is time to start the show.

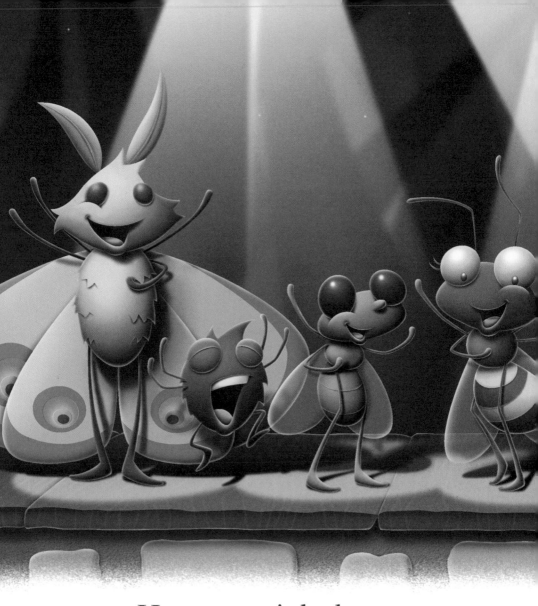

Here are eight bugs
who like to sing.
They all line up
from wing to wing.

One moth, one flea,
one fly, one bee.
One moth, one flea,
one fly, one bee.

Look over there!

Here come the ants.

They want to show off
their new dance.

They make a pattern
as they glide.

Hop, hop, slide!

Hop, hop, slide!

Now the fireflies
take flight.

They make bright loops
in the night.

The next act is
the best of all!
The bugs stack up
from big to small.

Six beetles, five spiders,
and four bees.
Three flies, two ants,
and one small flea.

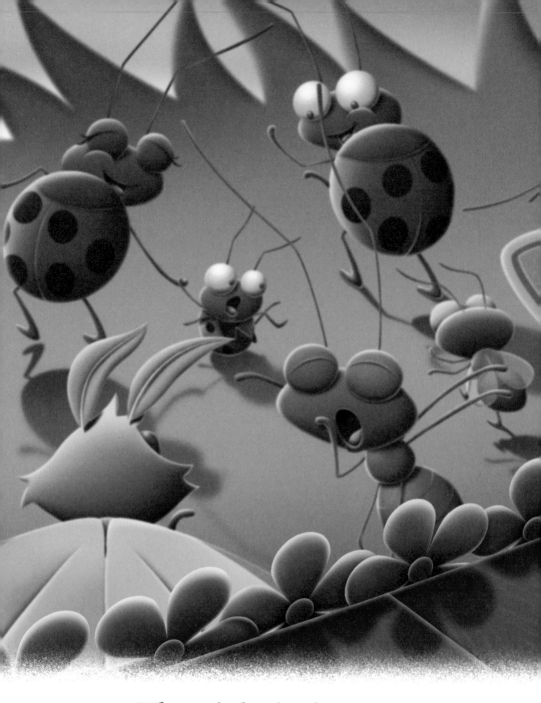

The night is done.

Here comes the sun!

The show is over.

The bugs had fun.

Now the busy bugs can rest.

The bug show really was the best!